Squirlish

The Girl in the Tree

CENTRAL PARK

GREAT LAWN

METRO-POLITAN MUSEUM OF ART

Squirrel Castle

Cordelia's Tree

Shakespeare's Grove

THE RAMBLE

THE LAKE

Squirrel Boat Pond

CENTRAL PARK WEST

CHERRY HILL

STRAWBERRY FIELDS

Touristy Lane

Ellen Potter

Squirlish

THE GIRL IN THE TREE

Art by Sara Cristofori

Margaret K. McElderry Books

New York   London   Toronto   Sydney   New Delhi

MARGARET K. McELDERRY BOOKS

An imprint of Simon & Schuster Children's Publishing Division
1230 Avenue of the Americas, New York, New York 10020

Text © 2023 by Ellen Potter
Illustrations © 2023 by Sara Cristofori
Jacket design by Rebecca Syracuse © 2023 by Simon & Schuster, Inc.

For information about special discounts for bulk purchases, please contact Simon & Schuster Special Sales at 1-866-506-1949 or business@simonandschuster.com.

The Simon & Schuster Speakers Bureau can bring authors to your live event. For more information or to book an event, contact the Simon & Schuster Speakers Bureau at 1-866-248-3049 or visit our website at www.simonspeakers.com.

Also available in a Margaret K. McElderry Books paperback edition.

Interior design by Rebecca Syracuse
The text for this book was set in Bookman Old Style Pro.
The illustrations for this book were rendered digitally.
Manufactured in the United States of America
0523 FFG
First Margaret K. McElderry Books hardcover edition June 2023
2 4 6 8 10 9 7 5 3 1
Library of Congress Cataloging-in-Publication Data · Names: Potter, Ellen, 1963- author. | Cristofori, Sara, illustrator. · Title: The girl in the tree / Ellen Potter ; art by Sara Cristofori. Description: First Margaret K. McElderry Books hardcover edition. | New York : Margaret K. McElderry Books, 2023. | Series: Squirlish | · Audience: Ages 6–9. | Audience: Grades 2–3. | Summary: Cordelia, a young girl raised by squirrels, tries to branch out from her squirrel family and make a human friend, but after stumbling into a gymnastics class she finds social skills are a tough nut to crack. · Identifiers: LCCN 2022054404 (print) | LCCN 2022054405 (ebook) | · ISBN 9781665926751 (hardcover) | ISBN 9781665926744 (paperback) | · ISBN 9781665926768 (ebook) · Subjects: CYAC: Squirrels—Fiction. | Friendship—Fiction. Classification: LCC PZ7.P8518 Gi 2023 (print) | LCC PZ7.P8518 (ebook) | · DDC [Fic]— dc23 · LC record available at https://lccn.loc.gov/2022054404 · LC ebook record available at https://lccn.loc.gov/2022054405

For my parents
—Ellen Potter

For Caterina and Emilio
—Sara Cristofori

1
The Girl in the Tree

Cordelia was a girl who lived in a tall elm tree in Central Park. No one knew where she came from. A squirrel named Shakespeare found her one evening under a shrub, when she was just a wee baby. Shakespeare didn't like the looks of this small human creature with its drippy nose and big staring eyes. He certainly had no intention of taking care of it. He enjoyed his alone time too much.

Some squirrels are like that.

Still, thought Shakespeare, *there is a coyote roaming around the park. A coyote might eat a human baby. Coyotes have no shame.*

Shakespeare hurried over to his neighbor, Miss Gertrude, an elderly squirrel who lived in the larch tree next door. Miss Gertrude was a very clever squirrel. When she saw the baby under the shrub,

she knew exactly what to do.

She found three strong pigeons. The pigeons each took a beakful of Cordelia's onesie and flew her straight up to an old squirrel's nest in Shakespeare's tree. The nest was big and sturdy enough for a small human baby. Cordelia curled up very comfortably and fell straight to sleep.

"But I don't want a baby," Shakespeare complained to Miss Gertrude. "Their noses run and their crying makes my ears feel all *buzzily*."

Shakespeare liked to make up new

words, like "buzzily" and "giggle-wig" and "minglebum."

"You found her for a reason, Shakespeare, even if you don't know what that reason is yet," declared Miss Gertrude. Then she turned and headed home to her larch tree, calling back, "Good night! I'll bring you some mashed acorns for her in the morning!"

Shakespeare climbed up his elm tree. He sat beside the nest and looked down at the little human creature. In her sleep, Cordelia reached out and held his tail, the way she might have held the hand of someone she trusted very much.

Shakespeare felt a little funny in his chest then. He thought it might have

been because of a bad walnut that he'd eaten. But later, much later, he realized why he had felt funny. It was because at that moment he knew Cordelia belonged to him, and he belonged to Cordelia . . . and *that* was simply *that.*

2
Nut Day!

It was a bright autumn morning in the park. Cordelia was curled up asleep in her tree house. She was eight years old now and had long since outgrown her nest. Shakespeare had built her a cozy tree house high up in the elm tree. In the winter it was as warm and snug as your own bedroom, and in the summer she could open a window and look up at the night stars.

The moment she awoke that morning, Cordelia remembered what day it was. She scurried out of her tree house, grabbed a branch, and swung herself to a limb lower down. Then just for fun, she did two somersaults across the narrow branch until she reached the trunk of the tree.

There was a large hole halfway up the tree trunk in which she kept all her stuff. She had a blue comb with a handle shaped like a mermaid. She had several good books, an old baseball, a chess piece shaped like a horse, and two stubs of chalk, one red and one purple. All her clothes were in the hole in the trunk too. It was surprisingly easy to find clothes in

Central Park, since parents were always leaving things behind at playgrounds. But she also had new clothes, which Viola Berry, the park's groundskeeper, gave her. She even had dress-up clothes—a football helmet and a unicorn headband and fairy wings.

Now she combed her hair with the mermaid comb. She put on a red-and-white-striped T-shirt and a pair of cargo pants with extra pockets. She was going to need them today!

After a moment's thought, she decided she should dress

up for the holiday, so she put on the football helmet and the fairy wings.

When she was done, she hopped lightly from branch to branch, as nimble as a circus performer on a tightrope, until she reached Shakespeare's nest.

"I'm ready," she said to Shakespeare. Shakespeare opened his eyes and twitched his whiskers. "Ready? For what?"

"Shakespeare," Cordelia said very severely, putting her hands on her hips. "Today is Nut Day."

"Is it Nut Day already?" he asked sleepily.

"Yes, and don't forget, you said I could choose the—" Cordelia looked around to make sure no one was listening, then lowered her voice. "The top secret place."

"Did I? Oh, I suppose I did. Okay, let me just stretch. . . ." He stretched very slowly and lazily, then he patted his rather large belly. "And I'll just give my paws a good cleaning. . . ."

"SHAKESPEARE!" Cordelia stamped her foot on the tree branch, making it tremble.

Shakespeare laughed. He'd only been teasing her. Then he leaped out of his nest. He was a fat squirrel but very agile. Zippity quick, both he and Cordelia scrambled down the tree and jumped to the ground.

It was so early in the morning that the only person around was Viola Berry, who lived in the groundskeeper's cottage next to the elm tree.

"Happy Nut Day, Cordelia!" Viola said. "The acorns are ripe and ready!"

Viola knew everything about Central Park. She knew which trees weren't feeling well and how to make them  feel better. She knew the secret places where the red-tailed hawks built their nests in the spring. She knew which hollowed-out trees held raccoons that cuddled together in the winter.

And she was the only person who knew that Cordelia lived in a tree.

"Wouldn't you like to live in a real house, Cordelia?" Viola once asked.

"I live in a tree house, which is even better," Cordelia replied.

"But wouldn't you like to live with a family?"

"Viola, I do live with a family! I have Shakespeare, and I have you, and I have all the squirrels in the whole entire neighborhood."

Viola understood every creature that lived in the park, and so she understood Cordelia, too. But still, she made sure that Cordelia had warm coats and blankets for the winter and new shoes for her growing feet. And though acorns and walnuts are fine for a squirrel, a human girl needs to eat other things as well. So Viola made sure that Cordelia had three meals a day, including dinner in Viola's cottage every night.

That morning, the squirrels were *everywhere*. They were darting between trees, leaping onto benches, and somersaulting in the grass. Nut Day is a big deal for squirrels. If you think about your favorite holiday and the bouncy way you feel when you wake up that morning, you'll understand what Nut Day is like for squirrels.

A small red squirrel named Bianca ran up to Cordelia. Waddling behind her was a young rat named Fenton.

"Good day and may you never have fleas!" Bianca said.

"Good day and may you never have fleas!" Cordelia replied, smiling.

This is the way all squirrels greet each other. If you go to Bulgaria or Senegal or

France, you'll find the squirrels there will greet each other exactly the same way.

"Play Dragon King with us, Cordelia," Fenton said.

Dragon King is a little like tag, but with more tree-climbing and tail-grabbing. No one ever wins or anything at Dragon King. The game is over when everyone is totally pooped out.

"Okay! I call Dragon King!" Cordelia shouted, and the chase was on. Cordelia raced after Bianca and Fenton, and when she caught Fenton, he chased Bianca. They were all having loads of fun, when suddenly Cordelia heard a snorty laugh from just above her head. She stopped running and looked up. Lounging on a tree branch was Bianca's older sister, Kate.

"What are you laughing at?" Cordelia asked her.

"You."

"Why?"

"Because you run like a human," said Kate.

"I do not!" Cordelia replied.

"Yes, you do. When you run, your arms go all *wonka-wonka-wonka*." Kate waved her paws around in a silly way.

Most of the time, Cordelia forgot she was a human. But when someone reminded her, like now, it made her feel all funny inside, like she'd swallowed a handful of earthworms.

"Don't pay any attention to her," Bianca told Cordelia. "Kate's the worst."

"She calls me a *rat*," Fenton said in a mopey way.

"You *are* a rat," Cordelia said.

"Yeah, but it's the *way* she says it," Fenton complained. "*Rrrat!* Like I eat garbage and stuff."

"You do eat garbage," Cordelia said truthfully.

"I eat *leftovers*," Fenton corrected her. "There's a difference."

They kept playing Dragon King, but the whole time Cordelia kept feeling those earthworms squirming in her belly.

3
You-Know-Whats

After the young squirrels were finished playing Dragon King, Cordelia watched the Fearless Five perform on the grassy lawn. The Fearless Five were five teenage boys who did acrobatics. The audience gasped and hooted and clapped each time one of the Fearless Five did a daring flip in the air.

That looks like fun, Cordelia thought. She wondered what it would feel like to be

one of the Fearless Five. Except for Viola,
she had no human friends. Cordelia was
curious about humans, but they also
made her feel shy and a little nervous.

"Ah, there you are, Cordelia!"
Shakespeare said as he trotted up to her.

"We'd better go hunting for nuts before the day gets away from us."

Hunting for nuts was the whole point of Nut Day. When the cold weather arrived, there would be no more fresh nuts or berries. On Nut Day, the squirrels had to collect as many nuts as they could and bury them in secret hiding spots. That way they'd be sure to have food to eat in the winter.

"Let's go find some—" Shakespeare looked all around him to see if any other squirrels were listening. "Let's go find some *you-know-whats*."

He didn't want to say the word "butter-nuts" out loud. That's because butternuts are squirrels' favorite sort of nuts. When the weather was *brrrr* and spring seemed like a million years away, there was nothing Shakespeare liked so much as a delicious butternut.

The neighborhood they lived in was called Shakespeare Grove. It was named after Shakespeare's great-great-great-great-grandfather, who was named after a very famous human writer. It was a beautiful neighborhood, with its own garden and an outdoor theater, where they put on many plays written by Shakespeare. (The *human* Shakespeare, not the *squirrel* Shakespeare.) It also had the only butternut tree in all of Central Park . . . and Shakespeare was the only squirrel who knew where that butternut tree was.

As Cordelia and Shakespeare walked to the butternut tree, they picked up acorns and an occasional walnut along the way.

"Hey, ho, one more for us!" Shakespeare would sing whenever he found a nut, and Cordelia would put the nut in a pocket of her cargo pants. Every so often, Cordelia let a few nuts fall out of her pockets, where one of her neighbors was sure to find them. After all, it wasn't really fair that Cordelia had pockets to store the nuts in, while all the other squirrels only had their cheeks.

The butternut tree was in a forgotten corner, right behind the Delacorte Theater. Shakespeare and Cordelia collected the small, green football-shaped butternuts. There were never as many as Shakespeare would have liked. Still, there were just enough to make a cold winter's night a little cozier.

"I choose the first hiding spot for the butternuts this year, remember?" Cordelia said.

"Lead the way, Captain!" Shakespeare cried. Pockets full of nuts always put him in an extra good mood.

Cordelia took him to the quiet little thicket where the trees grew snug together. She had discovered it one day while playing hide-and-seek with Fenton.

Shakespeare looked around.

"Well done, Cordelia," he said finally. "This is an excellent place to hide butter-nuts!"

Cordelia was filled with pride. Butternuts were valuable treasures, so choosing a hiding spot for them was a very important job.

Shakespeare began to dig the hole in the ground, his front paws working furi-ously.

All of a sudden, Cordelia got a spooky, goose-pimply feeling. It felt like someone was watching them.

"Shakespeare?" she said, looking all around. "Does that coyote still live in Central Park?"

"I think so," Shakespeare replied. "Butternuts, please."

Cordelia reached into her pocket, took out some of the butternuts, and dropped them into the hole. Then she nervously looked around the little thicket again. There were lots of shadows where a coyote could hide.

"Would a coyote eat a girl?" Cordelia asked.

"Not a girl as big as you," Shakespeare answered as he covered the butternuts with dirt.

"But a coyote would eat a squirrel, wouldn't it?" Cordelia asked.

Shakespeare paused. He didn't want to upset Cordelia. But he also always told her the truth about things.

"Yes, a coyote would eat a squirrel. But don't worry. I've got plenty of *smarticles*."

"What's that?" Cordelia asked.

"It means I avoid coyotes."

Shakespeare inspected his work, then waved his tail with satisfaction. "Done! Now let's find the next hiding spot!" He scurried out of the thicket and Cordelia followed him. But suddenly she stopped. That goose-pimply feeling had returned.

She grabbed a thick branch off the ground. If the coyote was nearby, she would scare it away with the stick. No squirrel-eating coyote was going to slink around her neighborhood!

There was a scuffling sound back in the thicket where they had buried the butternuts. Cordelia held her stick high, and as quietly as possible, she snuck back toward the

dense cluster of trees and shrubs. Then, with a loud cry of *"Ayiyiyiyi!"* she ran into the thicket.

But what she saw made her stop short and gasp!

4
Thief!

The hole they'd buried the butternuts in was all dug up. Their precious butternuts were gone! And standing by the empty hole was a squirrel with very bulgy cheeks.

The squirrel looked at Cordelia for a moment. His ears twitched and his tail flicked up and down. Then he turned around and ran like crazy.

"Thief!" Cordelia shouted, and she dashed after him.

She'd never been out of Shakespeare Grove in her entire life. As a rule, squirrels stay in their own neighborhoods. But this was an emergency.

The squirrel was fast, but so was she. He tried to lose Cordelia in a woodsy part of the park called the Ramble. The squirrel skittered beneath bushes and leapt over tree roots. Most humans would have given up the chase, but not Cordelia. She followed him through the woods, crashing through shrubs and ducking under low branches, staying right behind him.

When the woods ended, the squirrel darted into a crowd of people. For a moment, Cordelia lost sight of him.

"No, no, no!" she cried.

But then, on a statue of Alice in Wonderland, she saw the tip of a gray bushy tail peeking out above the brim of the Mad Hatter's hat.

In a flash, Cordelia scrambled up the statue.

"Got you!" she cried, reaching for the squirrel's tail. But the squirrel leapt off the statue before she could grab it. The chase was back on!

The squirrel ran down a busy path filled with tourists taking pictures and people sitting on benches. The squirrel jumped on the back of one of the benches.

People sitting on the bench screeched as he ran along its edge and then leapt to the next bench. It was a leap that only a squirrel could make. Well, a squirrel *and* Cordelia. Cordelia jumped onto the back of a bench and followed the thief. People stopped walking and watched in amazement as the girl in the football helmet and fairy wings leapt from bench to bench. When there were no more benches, the squirrel sprang into the air and landed on a tree branch. Cordelia followed right behind him. The two of them climbed the tree, higher and higher, until they reached the uppermost branch.

Now Cordelia had the squirrel trapped. He was at the tippy-top of the tree. There was nowhere else for him to go.

That's when the squirrel surprised Cordelia and made a daring leap to a nearby lamppost.

It was too far for Cordelia to jump. She knew she wouldn't make it. Still, she was determined to get those butternuts back!

Suddenly she had an idea. She grabbed a sturdy tree branch, took two mighty swings, one . . . two . . . and then she let go. She flew through the air, high over the heads of the people below her. Stretching out her arms, she grabbed hold of the lamppost just in time and hugged her arms and legs around it. After that it was easy to shimmy up to the very top, where the squirrel was perched.

"Give them back," she demanded, holding her palm under his mouth. "NOW!"

The squirrel knew when he was beaten. He made a short screech of annoyance, but he spit out the butternuts into her palm.

On the path below her, tourists had stopped to gawk up at her. As she slid

down the lamppost, they hooted and clapped. They assumed she was a street performer, like the Fearless Five.

Cordelia thought it was silly that everyone was so amazed by what she had done. She did things like that almost every day! It was all part of living in a tree. Still, when Cordelia reached the ground, she smiled and bowed, just like she'd seen the Fearless Five do at the end of their performance.

But Cordelia's smile faded when she saw a woman with short dark hair walk up to her. The woman looked very serious. Maybe climbing lampposts was against park rules.

"What's your name, little girl?" the stern-looking woman asked.

"Cordelia."

"Well, Cordelia, I'm Ms. Bird, and I need to speak to your parents. Immediately."

Uh-oh.

5
Cordelia Goes to School

Cordelia didn't know what to do. She couldn't tell the lady that she lived in a tree with a squirrel!

Looking around, Cordelia noticed a woman sitting on one of the benches. The woman was wearing purple pants and a purple hat. Perched on her shoulders were four squirrels, and at her feet was a sign that said TAKE A PICTURE WITH A REAL CENTRAL PARK SQUIRREL! $10.

Cordelia had heard about the squirrels in this part of the park, which was called Touristy Lane. Shakespeare said that the squirrels here were too friendly with people. He said that they would make fools of themselves for a peanut.

There was a long line of people standing beside the squirrel lady in the purple pants and hat. They were waiting to take a picture with a squirrel. A man in front of the line handed the squirrel lady a ten-dollar bill. He sat down on the bench and she placed a peanut on the man's shoulder. One of the squirrels on her shoulder hopped onto the man's shoulder and squatted there, eating the peanut while the man took a selfie.

Cordelia had an idea.

"My mother is over there," she said to Ms. Bird, pointing at the squirrel lady, "but she's too busy to talk now. You should probably come back later."

Cordelia didn't like to lie, but this seemed like an emergency.

Ms. Bird sniffed. "Nonsense," she said. To Cordelia's horror, Ms. Bird took Cordelia's hand and marched right over to the squirrel lady.

"Madam, I must speak to you," Ms. Bird said to the squirrel lady.

"Ten bucks for a selfie," Squirrel Lady replied. "Twenty if you want the squirrel to stand on your head. Go to the back of the line."

"I don't want a selfie," Ms. Bird said. "I want to talk to you about this child. I saw what she just did."

Oh no!

Cordelia tried to pull her hand out of Ms. Bird's so that she could make a run for it, but Ms. Bird held on tightly.

"She has tremendous talent," Ms. Bird continued.

Squirrel Lady narrowed her eyes at Cordelia. "She doesn't seem all that special to me."

"Not special?!" Ms. Bird cried. "She's a natural-born gymnast!"

"If you say so." Squirrel Lady shrugged.

Cordelia wasn't sure what Ms. Bird

was talking about, but at least she didn't seem mad about the lamppost.

Ms. Bird turned to Cordelia. "I am a coach at the American Academy of Gymnastics."

"The whatsy?" Cordelia asked.

"It's a school for young gymnasts."

A school?! Shakespeare had told Cordelia about school! He said that school was a place where human children went to learn things.

Of course Shakespeare did an excellent job of teaching Cordelia everything he knew. He took her to all the plays at the Delacorte Theater (they sat in a tree that overlooked the open-air theater and

could watch the plays perfectly from there). He taught her how to read (yes, some squirrels *can* read!), and how to count acorns, and even how to subtract and divide and multiply them. He taught her the names of all the different kinds of clouds in the sky and the flowers in the park. He taught her about the squirrels of Ancient Egypt, the Great Squirrel War of 1889, and about prehistoric flying squirrels that glided over the heads of dinosaurs.

Still, Cordelia often wondered about human school. Sometimes she thought it would be scary being around so many kids. But other times—especially when she saw groups of schoolchildren in the park for a field day—she thought school might be fun.

"What do you say, Cordelia?" Ms. Bird asked. "Would you like to go to our school?"

"I say . . ." Cordelia thought for a moment. Then she did a jump in the air, which is what young squirrels do when they're happy. "I say YES!"

Ms. Bird turned to Squirrel Lady and

said, "Do I have your permission to take Cordelia to my school? She can spend the afternoon there and see how she likes it."

"Sure." Squirrel Lady shrugged. "Whatever floats your boat."

6
Ambush!

The American Academy of Gymnastics was just a few blocks away from the park. Cordelia skipped alongside Ms. Bird, excited by all the sights of the city. There were so many cars and buses and stores! Cordelia had never been outside of the park before. She tried to memorize everything she saw, so that she could tell Shakespeare all about it when she got back home.

The academy was in a shiny building with giant glass doors. They walked down a long, polished hallway that made Cordelia's shoes squeak and then went into a large room covered in squishy blue and red mats.

"Welcome to the American Academy of Gymnastics," Ms. Bird said.

The room was filled with fun-looking things. There were bars high off the

ground that you could do flips on, and thick mats to bounce on and tumble across. There was even a big pit full of spongy foam bricks that you could jump into.

But most amazing of all, there were kids! Lots of them!

Ms. Bird led Cordelia over to a group

of girls and boys who looked like they were around Cordelia's age. "You can do warm-ups with these children, Cordelia. I'll be back soon."

The kids stared at Cordelia's football helmet and fairy wings.

Cordelia suddenly felt very shy. She knew how to make friends with other squirrels. That was easy. You just chased each other around and around until you were friends. But these kids weren't running and playing like young squirrels. They looked very serious as they touched their toes and did arm circles.

One girl stopped stretching for a moment and walked up to Cordelia. Her heart began to thud with excitement and nervousness. A kid was going to talk to her!

"How come you're wearing a football helmet and fairy wings?" the girl asked.

"Because it's Nut Day," Cordelia said gleefully.

"It sure is," the girl muttered to another girl, and the two of them smiled at each other. They were not nice smiles, either. Cordelia might not have known any human kids, but she could tell a making-fun-of-someone smile when she saw one. She quickly took off her helmet and fairy wings.

Cordelia's cheeks felt hot with embarrassment. Now more than ever, she wished she were a squirrel with a furry face. Furry faces didn't turn red when they were embarrassed.

Stupid no-hair skin face! she thought to herself angrily. She looked away from those girls so they couldn't see her turning colors.

It was then that she noticed a girl who was standing on a long, narrow red mat. The girl had a bushy black ponytail. Cordelia thought her ponytail looked a lot like a squirrel's tail.

Suddenly the girl raised her arms, took a running leap, flipped completely upside down two times, and landed on her feet again.

Cordelia had *never* seen a human child do something like that before! Even the Fearless Five couldn't do two flips in a row!

"Good job, Annabeth," one of the coaches said to the girl with the ponytail.

Annabeth smiled. It was a nice smile.

Annabeth would be the perfect friend for me! Cordelia thought. She imagined playing with Annabeth in the park. Cordelia could show her all the best trees to climb. They could swing from the branches and do flips in the grass and have a great time.

So Cordelia did what young squirrels always do when they want to become friends with another squirrel. She skipped over to Annabeth, bared her teeth, and chattered them loudly while she jumped up and down.

At first, Annabeth looked so surprised that she didn't move. She just stared back at Cordelia with big eyes. Then Annabeth turned and ran.

Yes! thought Cordelia. *The chase is on!*

Annabeth dashed off the mat with Cordelia right behind, making barking noises at her.

The other kids in the gym stopped what they were doing to watch this strange turn of events. Some of the kids cheered.

"STOP, STOP!" cried one of the coaches.

But it's hard for young squirrels to stop chasing once they've started. And even though Cordelia wasn't *really* a squirrel, she had always lived with squirrels, so of course she acted like one too.

Cordelia chased Annabeth all around the gym. Cordelia knew she could catch her. If she reached out her hand, she could grab the tip of Annabeth's bushy, squirrelly ponytail. But chasing was the fun part, not catching.

Cordelia spotted a tall stack of blue gym mats. She clambered up them. When she got to the top, she stood up tall, spread her arms like wings, and jumped off.

"AMBUSH!" she yelled, flying through the air.

Annabeth shrieked as Cordelia landed right in front of her and chattered her teeth at her happily.

"Cordelia!" Ms. Bird marched up to her looking very angry. "We do not act like wild animals here. Now, apologize to Annabeth."

Cordelia looked at Annabeth in confusion. She had thought that Annabeth was having fun. But now she could see that Annabeth was staring at her with angry eyes.

"I'm sorry," she said to Annabeth quietly.

Annabeth just glared at her in silence before she turned and walked away.

It didn't seem like Cordelia and Annabeth would be friends after all.

How do human children ever become friends if they don't chase each other first? Cordelia wondered. It was a mystery. And now she was feeling those darn earthworms squirming in her belly again.

7
Disaster

Ms. Bird told Cordelia that she would begin with the basics. She pointed at a plank of wood that was only a few inches off the floor.

"That is a balance beam. Let's see you walk across it," Ms. Bird said.

This seemed like a silly thing to do. Cordelia walked across tree branches every day. Those branches were narrower than the beam, and much higher off the ground. Still, Shakespeare had told her that in school, the children had to listen to the teacher. Cordelia stepped up on the beam and walked across it.

"Good!" said Ms. Bird. "Now walk across the beam twenty more times."

Ms. Bird turned her attention to another student while Cordelia walked back and forth across the beam. After the fourth time, she got bored and did a high jump in the air, landing neatly back on the beam. A few kids who were sitting on the floor noticed.

"That new girl can jump high!" one of them said.

This boosted Cordelia's spirits. She did another jump in the air, higher this time.

Now a bunch of kids were staring at her with interest.

Maybe this was how human children became friends.

Across the room, Cordelia spotted

a boy in green shorts who was flipping around on a bar high off the ground. He flipped twice around the bar then he flew into the air and landed in the deep pit full of squishy foam blocks.

If they like my jumps on the balance beam, Cordelia thought, *wait until they see what I can do on that high bar!*

"Hey, look at this!" Cordelia said to the kids who were sitting on the floor.

She hopped off the wooden beam and ran over to the bar. Leaping up, she grabbed the bar. Then she swung her feet and spun around the bar super fast.

She checked to see if the kids sitting on the floor were watching her. They were.

But *uh-oh*, Ms. Bird was watching her too.

"Cordelia!" Ms. Bird called. "Come down from there! You are supposed to be on the balance beam!"

"But the balance beam is so boring!" Cordelia called back.

Cordelia spun around the bar once, twice, then she let go, tucked her legs in, and flipped three times in the air.

Everyone gasped.

"She's doing a triple back dismount!" one girl cried out.

Even the coaches were watching in amazement. They had never seen any of their gymnasts do that before.

Squiiiish! Cordelia landed in the foam pit, smiling wide. All the kids cheered. Well, all the kids *except* for the boy in the green shorts. He was in the foam pit too, looking worried.

"Some stuff fell out of your pockets," the boy told Cordelia. "I think they were nuts."

8
Chittering

Cordelia felt around in her pockets. They were all empty. The nuts must have fallen out of her pockets and into the foam pit while she had done her flips!

She looked at the foam bricks all around her. There were no signs of the nuts anywhere. They must have sunk to the bottom of the deep pit and were now buried under dozens and dozens of foam bricks.

"No, no, no, no!" cried Cordelia. She started to dig though the bricks, when she heard a stern voice above her.

"Cordelia!"

Cordelia looked up. Ms. Bird was frowning down at her from the edge of the pit.

"You are a talented girl, Cordelia. One day you could be a great gymnast," said Ms. Bird. "But you are obviously not ready for our school. Come out of the pit. I'm taking you back to your mother."

"I have to find my stuff first!" Cordelia said as she dug more frantically. But each time she tossed one brick aside, another foam brick toppled into its place.

"We're leaving," Ms. Bird said firmly. *"Now."*

Cordelia sighed miserably. There was nothing else to do. She climbed out of the pit. With her head hung low, she grabbed her helmet and fairy wings and followed Ms. Bird out of the school, across the street, and back to the park.

Ms. Bird marched Cordelia straight back to the squirrel lady.

"I'm afraid it didn't work out," Ms. Bird said to the lady.

Squirrel Lady grunted. "I'm not surprised."

This had been the worst day of Cordelia's life. Not only had she been kicked out of school, but she'd lost all their nuts. What would Shakespeare eat all winter? They'd have to scrounge around for any puny leftover acorns that the other squirrels didn't want. Just the thought of telling Shakespeare the bad news when she got back home made her stomach hurt.

Then she realized something. She

wasn't even sure *how* to get back home!

"Excuse me," Cordelia said to a sleek squirrel with a well-groomed tail, who was having her photo taken on a teenage girl's shoulder. "How do I get back to Shakespeare Grove?"

Cordelia asked this in Chittering, the official squirrel language. Chittering is a very difficult language to learn, much harder than any language humans speak. It has lots of clicks and clacks and barks and squeals.

"Whoa!" cried the sleek squirrel. "You can, like, speak Chittering! Wait! Wait! Wait! Are you . . . ?" The squirrel leapt off the girl's shoulder and ran over to Cordelia. "Yes, I think you ARE! You're Cordelia!"

"Yes," Cordelia answered hesitantly. She wondered how the squirrel knew who she was.

"Okay, I'm going to, like, pass out! Hey, everyone!" the squirrel called out to the other squirrels. "There's a celebrity here!"

"Big deal, Gracie!" said a squirrel who had been gnawing on a pizza crust one of the tourists had tossed to him. "We see celebrities here every day."

"No, you guys, this is a *real* celebrity! This is CORDELIA!"

9
The Most Famous Girl in Central Park

The other squirrels stopped what they were doing and rushed over to Cordelia.

"It's her!" one cried.

"We thought you weren't real! We thought you were just a myth," said another one.

"Can I have some of your hair for my nest?" another asked excitedly.

"Ooh, me too! Me too!"

And then a half dozen squirrels began

to climb up on Cordelia to pull out some of her hair, but she shook them off like a dog shaking off bathwater.

"You can't take my hair," she told them firmly. "I need it for my head. Anyway, how do all of you know who I am? I've never even been outside of Shakespeare Grove before."

"You're the Squirrel Girl of Central Park! You're famous! Every squirrel in the whole park knows about the girl who lives in a tree," Gracie told her. "Every squirrel in the whole, like, entire city knows about you!"

By now there was a sea of squirrels surrounding Cordelia, circling her feet excitedly.

"Look at that girl with all the squirrels!"
tourists cried, and they began to take
pictures of her. Everyone was delighted.
Everyone *except* for the squirrel lady. She
was not happy at all. Cordelia was taking
away her squirrels, which meant Cordelia
was taking away her business.

"Police! Police!" Squirrel Lady shouted. "This child is disturbing all the squirrels!"

Several yards away, a policewoman heard her shouts and headed over.

Uh-oh.

Cordelia started to walk away quickly, which is very difficult when you have hundreds of squirrels all around your feet.

"Excuse me, excuse me, oops, sorry . . ." A few tails were stepped on as Cordelia walked in a zigzag, which is how squirrels walk when they are trying to escape danger.

But the squirrels wouldn't leave her side. They zigzagged right along with her.

"We'll show you the way back to Shakespeare Grove," Gracie said.

And so Cordelia was escorted through Central Park by a large group of excited, babbling Touristy Lane squirrels. When they reached the Boat Pond, the Touristy Lane squirrels handed Cordelia over to the Boat Pond squirrels (squirrels don't like leaving their own neighborhoods, so the Touristy Lane squirrels went straight back home). The Boat Pond squirrels had jumped right off their homemade boats and swam to shore when they heard Cordelia was approaching! As they led her through the park, they sang songs about pond monsters and mermaids, and they asked if she'd be the guest of honor at their next Pirate Festival. Cordelia happily accepted. When they reached the Metropolitan Museum of Art, the Museum Hill squirrels took over. The Museum Hill squirrels tried to act dignified about the

whole thing, but one of them managed to gnaw off a bit of Cordelia's shoelaces to display in his next art exhibit. When they arrived at Belvedere Castle, the Squirrel Queen sent out her best knights, who rode on the backs of enormous snapping turtles, to escort Cordelia the rest of the way home. This was the slowest part of the journey, of course, because . . . you know . . . turtles. But finally, Cordelia arrived at her very own elm tree, where she found Shakespeare waiting. And he didn't look happy.

10
Isaac

"What on earth?" Shakespeare said, as he watched the squirrel knights bow to Cordelia, then head back (slowly) to Belvedere Castle.

"Shakespeare," Cordelia said excitedly, "all the squirrels in the park know who I am!"

"Do they really?" He was as surprised as Cordelia. But then he remembered that

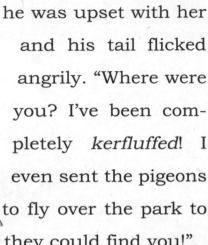

he was upset with her and his tail flicked angrily. "Where were you? I've been completely *kerfluffed*! I even sent the pigeons to fly over the park to see if they could find you!"

There had been so much going on during her walk home that Cordelia had nearly forgotten about her disastrous day. Now she sighed, sat on the ground beside Shakespeare, and told him the whole sad story. When she got to the part about the nuts that fell out of her pockets, Shakespeare gasped. He didn't mean to; it just came out. That made Cordelia cry, she felt so bad. So he climbed onto her shoulder and tickled her chin with his tail.

"*Shh*, don't worry, Cordelia. It will be okay," he told her gently.

"But you'll have nothing to eat this winter," she moaned.

"Nonsense. I'm sure we'll find some acorns. And maybe even a few walnuts. Nut Day isn't over yet. Now tell me, Cordelia," he said to change the subject and cheer her up, "what was human school like? Did you learn anything interesting?"

Cordelia sniffed, then shook her head.

"They just made me walk on a piece of wood, back and forth, back and forth, about a million times. And then I got into trouble. . . . Oh, Shakespeare, I don't fit in anywhere. I'm not good at being a girl, but I'm not a squirrel, either. So what am I?"

It was a good question, and Shakespeare was thinking about how to answer when they heard a voice behind them:

"Um, excuse me."

Cordelia and Shakespeare turned around to see a boy wearing green sweatpants.

"I know you," Cordelia

said to him, standing up and wiping her eyes. "You did the flip into the foam pit."

The boy nodded. "I'm Isaac." He held out a brown paper bag. "I think these are yours."

Cordelia took the bag and looked inside.

"The nuts!" Cordelia cried. "Thank you. But how did you get them?"

"I volunteered to clean out the foam pit so that I could find them for you. Everyone hates cleaning out that pit. There's all kinds of gross stuff at the bottom, like Band-Aids and chewed gum."

Cordelia turned to Shakespeare, holding out the open bag. "Look, Shakespeare!

He brought them back! All of them!"

"How kind," Shakespeare said stiffly. Like most squirrels (except for the ones who like to have their selfies taken), Shakespeare was a little suspicious of humans.

Isaac watched as Cordelia made the strange clicking and growling sounds to Shakespeare. When Shakespeare made those strange noises back to her, Isaac's eyes widened with surprise.

"Were you just talking to that squirrel?" he asked Cordelia.

"Of course," Cordelia said.

"Can you teach me how to say something in squirrel?" Isaac asked.

"It's called Chittering, and it's kind of hard to learn," she warned him.

"Oh, I'm good with languages," Isaac assured her. "I can say all the days of the week in Spanish."

So Cordelia taught Isaac how to say the Chittering greeting. "Good day and may you never have fleas."

After practicing a few times, Isaac knelt down in front of Shakespeare.

"What's he doing?" Shakespeare asked Cordelia nervously.

"He's going to talk to you," she replied, then added, "Be nice, Shakespeare."

"Good day and may you never have fleas," Isaac told Shakespeare.

Except it came out all wrong.

"Did that boy just say, 'Your nose hairs need a trim'?" Shakespeare asked Cordelia.

Cordelia nodded.

"What did the squirrel say back?" Isaac asked Cordelia excitedly.

"He said . . . he said he hopes you never have fleas either."

Isaac pounded his chest proudly. "I speak squirrel!"

11
Nose Hairs

"Hey, I just thought of something," Cordelia said to Isaac. "How did you know where to find me?"

"Oh, I see you here all the time," Isaac replied. He pointed at the five teenagers who were tumbling in front of an audience across the lawn. "Those are my brothers."

"The Fearless Five? I love those guys!"

"They say when I'm a little bigger, I

can be part of their act. But for now, I just have to get better at my back handspring."

"What's that?" Cordelia asked.

After Isaac explained that a back handspring was a backward flip, Cordelia swatted her hand in the air and said, "Oh, those? Those are easy! I'll show you."

Cordelia and Isaac practiced their back handsprings on the grass. Isaac kept falling sideways but after about a dozen times, he managed to do a pretty decent one.

They were talking and laughing and having such a good time that Cordelia suddenly realized something.

"Are we friends now?" she asked Isaac.

"I think so," said Isaac.

"But we didn't chase each other or anything," Cordelia said.

"We *can* chase each other," Isaac offered. "I mean, if you really want to."

Cordelia considered this. It seemed like making friends with humans happened mysteriously. You just suddenly felt like you had a million more things to talk about with that person and a zillion more fun things that you wanted to do with that person.

"No, we don't need to chase each other," Cordelia said. "Let's go watch the Fearless Five!"

As they walked, Isaac crouched down whenever he saw a squirrel and said to it, "Good day and may you never have fleas."

Or at least, his version of it.

He said "Good day and may you never have fleas" to Bianca, who giggled. He started to say "Good day and may you never have fleas" to Fenton, too, but when Isaac saw he was a rat, he made a face and backed away.

"He doesn't care about *my* nose hairs, just because I'm a rat," complained Fenton, who spoke Chittering very well.

But when Isaac heard Fenton squeak so sadly, he knelt down and said, "Good day and may you never have fleas" to him, too.

Fenton was thrilled. "Oh yes, I'll trim my nose hairs right away, right away!" he replied.

Isaac would have said "Good day and

may you never have fleas" to Kate, but she started throwing acorns at him before he had the chance.

He even said "Good day and may you never have fleas" to Miss Gertrude, who was enjoying a bit of shade beneath her larch tree after a long day of collecting nuts. Miss Gertrude's tail twitched in surprise. Then she scurried over to Shakespeare.

"The most extraordinary thing just happened," Miss Gertrude said. "That boy over there told me that my nose hairs needed trimming."

"Cordelia's trying to teach him Chittering," Shakespeare explained as he watched Cordelia and Isaac with a worried look on his face. "Do you think it's good for her to have human friends?"

Miss Gertrude was quiet for a moment. Then she said, "Every once in a while, a human will find a baby squirrel who is all alone. And that human will take the baby squirrel home and feed it and keep it warm and safe."

"That's very kind of them," Shakespeare said.

"Yes, it is," agreed Miss Gertrude. "And if the human is *very* wise, they will help the baby squirrel learn how to do squirrelly things, like how to climb trees and find acorns and play with other squirrels. Because one day, that baby squirrel will grow into a big squirrel and it may want to live with other squirrels instead of humans."

Shakespeare thought about this. He felt a sad little lump in his throat as he said, "I suppose one day Cordelia might want to live with other people instead of us squirrels."

"Maybe," Miss Gertrude said gently. "Not for a very long time, of course. But maybe someday."

"In that case, it's probably good for her to do human-ish things," Shakespeare said bravely. "Like playing with other children."

"You are a very wise squirrel," said Miss Gertrude.

"Thank you, Miss Gertrude. And I think your nose hairs look perfect just the way they are."

12
Shakespeare in the Park

That night, Cordelia snuggled into bed in her tree house and told Shakespeare all about Isaac.

"He has five brothers and he lives in Brooklyn and he sleeps in a bunk bed, which is sort of like sleeping in a tree. And tomorrow he's going to show me how to ride a skateboard and I'm going to teach him more Chittering."

"I'm glad you made a human friend," Shakespeare said. "You've been around squirrels for so long, I sometimes forget that you're a girl, not a squirrel."

That made Cordelia frown. "I'm a *little* bit squirrel," she said. She thought for a moment. "I'm . . . *squirlish!*"

"Cordelia!" Shakespeare exclaimed with delight. "You made up your own word!"

"I guess that runs in the family," said Cordelia.

"I guess it does," Shakespeare agreed.

Shakespeare told Cordelia a story about a squirrel who was shipwrecked on an enchanted island, and afterward

Cordelia lay awake in her tree house, listening to the sounds of Central Park. She heard Miss Gertrude snoring in the tree next door. She heard the hoot of an owl and the quivery *coo-coo* of a pigeon. And somewhere (far, far away, she hoped) she heard the howl of that mysterious coyote.

The world is a big place, she thought. *It's full of islands and bunk beds and foam pits and Brooklyn.* But if she had to choose someplace to be—the best place of all—she would still choose to be right where she was . . . with Shakespeare in the park.

Acknowledgments

Cordelia and Shakespeare are the dream team. I feel the same way about all the brilliant people who helped create this series. I am so grateful to my editor, Karen Wojtyla, who is as word-wise as Shakespeare (both the squirrel and the human version). Thanks to Nicole Fiorica and the whole Squirlish Squad at Margaret K. McElderry Books for their enthusiasm and guidance. As always, I'm forever and always indebted to my extraordinary agent, Alice Tasman. Thanks to illustrator Sara Cristofori, who brought Cordelia, Shakespeare, and all the Central Park squirrels to life in the most delightful way. I'm so grateful for the insight of Squirlish's early readers, Kimberley Gorelik and Gabe and Millie Boscana. Finally, thanks to Adam and Ian, my precious touchstones.